ALIEN FOR RENT

Betsy Duffey

A Yearling Book

Published by
Dell Yearling
an imprint of
Random House Children's Books
a division of Random House, Inc.
1540 Broadway
New York, New York 10036

Visit us on the Web! www.randomhouse.com/kids

Educators and librarians, for a variety of teaching tools, visit us at www.randomhouse.com/teachers

ISBN: 0-440-41468-7

Reprinted by arrangement with Delacorte Press

Printed in the United States of America

May 2000

10 9 8 7 6 5 4 3 2 1

CWO

*For the students, teachers, and faculty
at High Point School, with thanks*

Contents

1

No Such Things?

"There are no such things as aliens," J.P. said. He stood with Lexie in the hall of the school and stared at a sign on the bulletin board.

"I'm not so sure," said Lexie. "Look."

Most of the signs said things like TRUMPET FOR SALE and BABY-SITTING and GARAGE SALE TOMORROW.

This sign was different. It was larger than the others and it glowed a ghostly green color.

The sign said ALIEN FOR RENT.

J.P. rubbed his eyes and looked more closely at

the strange sign. The letters were silver and seemed to float on the paper.

J.P. didn't like things that were different, things he couldn't understand. He liked things to stay the same. Like the lunch his mother packed every day—a zucchini sandwich and three carrot sticks, always the same.

J.P. touched the paper. The letters were warm. It was definitely different.

"This has to be a joke," he said. "I'm sure there are no such things as aliens."

"Hmmm," Lexie said. "I don't know. Read it out loud." She was excited.

" 'Alien for rent,' " J.P. began reading. " 'Can hire by the hour or day.' "

He stopped and looked at Lexie. "Did you put that up there?" he asked. "It's another one of your jokes, right? Like the time you told everyone the ice cream freezer in the cafeteria was broken and there was free ice cream?"

"That was a good joke." She laughed. "But this is not one of my jokes."

"How about the time you dressed up like a new kid and tried to fool Mr. Cleaver?"

"That was a good one too. But this is not a joke. I really didn't do it this time. Read more."

" 'Two gugentocks per hour,' " he read. "Gugentocks? What's a gugentock?"

"I have no idea. Must be some kind of alien money."

"Someone is playing a joke on us," said J.P. "I want to find out who it is. Is there a phone number?"

"No," said Lexie. "But it has a place to meet him."

"Or her," said J.P.

"Or it."

" 'Meet me at the third tree on the ground of play,' " J.P. read. "He means the playground."

Lexie giggled. "It *is* pretty funny. It's almost time for recess. Only five more minutes. I'll wait for you on the playground and we can go to the third tree together."

J.P. nodded. "Bring your gugentocks," he said.

Lexie laughed. "Don't tell anyone," she said.

"Tell anyone what?" a voice called out.

"Oh no," said J.P. "It's Bruce."

A large boy walked along the hall toward them. He had a purple streak in his hair. His T-shirt said BE AFRAID. "Hey, babies," he said. He flexed his muscles a few times as he walked.

Bruce was a fifth-grader. He was mean to everyone who was smaller than he was, especially third-graders like Lexie and J.P. "What's up?"

"Nothing, Bruce." They began to back away. Bruce was trouble.

"What do you mean, nothing? Tell me what you were talking about. Or else." He slammed his fist into his hand. He took a step forward. He raised his fist.

Mr. Cleaver walked out of the cafeteria. Bruce's fist went down.

"Mr. Cleaver!" Lexie called out to him. "Over here." It was the first time all year that she had been happy to see the principal.

"Hall passes," he demanded.

Lexie and J.P. had been on their way to the me-

4

dia center when they had seen the sign. They had hall passes. Lexie's pass was crumpled in a ball. She smoothed it out on her knee and held it up for Mr. Cleaver to see. J.P. pulled his out of his pocket. It was neat and flat.

Bruce looked at the floor. No hall pass.

"Come on to the office." Mr. Cleaver took Bruce's arm and frowned. "Again."

Mr. Cleaver looked at Lexie and J.P. "You two, back to class."

Bruce glared at them as he walked away. "Later," he mouthed.

"Oooo boy!" J.P. said. "Now Bruce is mad at us. He said one time that he had an unhappy childhood. Now he's trying to make everybody else's childhood unhappy."

"Yeah," said Lexie. "Like ours."

They turned to leave. "Let's take that sign down," J.P. said. "So no one else will see it."

"Good idea." Lexie reached up to get the sign. "That's weird," she said.

"What?" J.P. looked up at the bulletin board.

The spot where the card had been was still glowing a ghostly green. But the sign was gone.

"There are no such things as aliens," said J.P. But he no longer sounded so sure of himself.

"I guess we'll find out in a few minutes," said Lexie. Her eyes sparkled with excitement. "Alien, here we come."

2

Earthling Calling Alien

"One, two, three." Lexie counted down the trees on the playground. "Here's where we meet him."

"Or her," J.P. said.

"Or it."

A breeze blew the branches. The leaves made a rustling noise. They dropped their lunch boxes under the tree and began to look around.

Nothing.

They looked up into the branches as far as possible.

Nothing.

They sat down under the tree to wait. "We have twenty minutes before lunch," Lexie said. "I hope it's enough time."

"I knew there were no such things as aliens," said J.P. "For one thing, someone would have seen them land."

"The weatherman said on the news this morning that there were a lot of shooting stars last night."

"Well," J.P. said, "if there was really an alien, why would he come to school? He should go to the White House or to the space center."

"Someone has to be the first to see him," said Lexie. "Why not us?"

A small spider lowered itself on a single thread of its web. Lexie looked closely at the spider.

"Hello," she said softly. "Earthling calling alien." She put her nose right up to the spider.

The spider didn't answer. It crawled back up the thread.

"I guess that wasn't it," said Lexie.

A squirrel paused beside the tree to eat a nut. "Earthling calling alien," Lexie said to the squirrel.

The squirrel didn't answer. He ran up the tree with his nut.

"I guess that wasn't it either."

Lexie looked at the ground. It was covered with acorns. She picked up an acorn from beneath the tree and held it in her palm.

"Earthling calling alien. You in there?"

No answer.

"What are you guys doing?" a voice asked from behind the tree. "Talking to your relatives?"

Bruce walked out from behind the tree.

Lexie gave him a hard look. "You did it, right?" she said.

Bruce looked blank. "Did what?" he asked.

"Come on," said J.P. "Admit it. Gugentocks? Remember?"

"You guys are such babies," Bruce said. "I came over to teach you a lesson. You got me in trouble today."

"Sorry," Lexie said.

"Sorry is not enough."

"Double sorry?" J.P. tried.

Bruce moved closer.

His face was red and angry. He stepped in front of J.P.

"Triple sorry?" J.P. said in a tiny voice.

Bruce did not answer, but his hand began to form a fist. It was a large fist.

"Better not hit me," J.P. said. "My mother doesn't like me to get my clothes wrinkled."

"Too bad for your mother," Bruce said. He swung his fist toward J.P.'s stomach.

"Somebody stop him!" Lexie yelled.

The fist stopped in midswing. Bruce froze like a statue. He seemed to glow—green. His body rose about two inches off the ground.

"What's going on?" Bruce said. His eyes widened with fear. "What are you doing to me?" J.P. backed away and stood by Lexie.

"We're not doing anything," Lexie said.

"Let me down." Bruce sounded scared. "I can't move."

Lexie and J.P. took a step backward, never taking their eyes off Bruce.

"He's green," J.P. said. He gripped Lexie's arm. He was trembling.

"He's frozen," Lexie said. She gripped back.

"It's like something on TV."

Lexie looked at Bruce. "Go away," she said.

Whatever was holding Bruce seemed to let him go. He dropped to the ground, then crawled away a few steps before he broke into a run.

Lexie's mouth dropped open. She couldn't believe what she had just seen. She should have been speechless, but Lexie was never speechless. She always had to have the last word. As she watched Bruce run away she couldn't resist yelling, "You're the baby!"

She turned to J.P. He was still shaking.

"What happened?" he said. "One minute I was about to get a knuckle sandwich. The next minute Bruce got green."

"Something made Bruce act that way," said Lexie. "That something is around here somewhere."

"Let's get out of here," J.P. said. "That something might get us next."

Lexie didn't listen. She began to look around her. "Earthling calling alien," she said.

"I don't want to turn green," J.P. said.

"Shhhhhh," Lexie said. "Earthling calling alien."

"Green's not my color."

"Earthling calling alien."

They walked around the tree and back to their lunch boxes.

"Oooo boy!" J.P. said.

Lexie's lunch box was glowing a ghostly green.

3
Alien Burps

*B*urrrp!

A noise came from the lunch box.

J.P. and Lexie slowly moved closer. They stopped a few feet away.

"Did you hear something?" J.P. asked.

Lexie nodded. "I don't know for sure, but I think it was a burp."

"An alien burp?"

Lexie nodded again.

They stared at the lunch box. They listened very hard for a few moments.

Lexie started forward. J.P. pulled her back.

"I don't think we should open it," he said. "I think we should call someone."

"Who?"

"Someone like the fire department. Or the bomb squad. Or my mother."

Lexie thought for a moment. "It would take so long for someone to come."

"I don't mind waiting," J.P. said.

Lexie shook her head. "I've never been very good at waiting."

She moved a little closer. She touched the lunch box very gently with her foot.

Burp!

Another noise came out of the lunch box. Lexie jumped back.

"I did hear something that time," J.P. said. "And it was definitely a burp. An alien burp."

Lexie nodded.

"I saw a movie on TV," J.P. said, "where aliens ate humans for breakfast."

They stared at the lunch box.

"Well," Lexie said. She thought for a moment. "I

think that if it's looking for food in a lunch box, it probably doesn't eat people."

"I saw another movie," J.P. said, "where aliens took a man away in a spaceship."

Lexie looked a little worried. She thought for a moment. "I think that if it can fit in that lunch box, its spaceship would be too small for us," she said finally.

They heard the sound of paper crinkling. They heard smacking noises.

"In one movie they turned everyone into giant plants."

"Oh?"

"In one they took over the White House."

"Oh?"

"In one they drank all the gasoline on the planet."

Lexie frowned. "I think you watch too much TV. Whatever is in there is not eating humans or drinking gasoline. It's eating my lunch!"

"Let him eat it," said J.P. "He can have my lunch

too. Like a peace offering, you know, a sign of goodwill between planets."

"That's easy for you to say," said Lexie. "You've got a zucchini sandwich and carrot sticks. My mother packed Twinkies."

She rolled up her sleeves. "No one's eating my Twinkies," she said in a determined voice.

"Not even as a sign of goodwill?"

"Nope." She shook her head.

"Not even for world peace?"

"Nope."

J.P. stepped back. He closed his eyes. He covered them with his hands.

Lexie stepped forward.

She leaned down.

Her hand paused just above the lunch box.

The lunch box glowed.

Lexie took a deep breath.

She pulled on the zipper.

She eased the top open.

A-A-A-Alien!

"A-A-A-Alien!" Lexie screamed. She grabbed J.P.'s arm.

"I can't look," J.P. said. "We're going to die."

They jumped up and down and screamed together.

"A-A-A-Alien," Lexie said again. She squeezed J.P.'s arm even tighter. "Look, J.P.," she said. "Tell me if I'm dreaming."

J.P. shook his head. "I can't look," he said. "I know we're going to die. Does it look dangerous?"

Lexie looked at the lunch box again.

She stopped jumping up and down.

"Is it big and disgusting?" J.P. asked.

"No." Lexie let go of his arm. "Not too disgusting." She bent down to look closer. "Actually, it's small and kind of cute."

"Cute? Aliens are supposed to be big and disgusting, not cute."

"And it's kind of chubby."

"Aliens are definitely not supposed to be chubby. They're supposed to be thin and silver."

"Well, this one is chubby and green and kind of . . . well . . . fuzzy."

"They're supposed to be slimy."

"No slime," Lexie said.

"What's he doing?" asked J.P. "Is he going to zap us with laser beams? Is he going to liquidate us? Is he going to—"

"I don't know for sure. But I think he's asleep."

"Asleep! You mean we're not going to die?" J.P. dropped his hands from his eyes and leaned forward.

In the lunch box was a small, cute, chubby, fuzzy, green creature lying on top of Lexie's peanut butter sandwich. Beside the creature was an empty Twinkies wrapper. The creature slept on its back and made soft snoring noises.

Hum brum brum brum.

Hum brum brum brum.

As they watched, the creature opened its eyes. It looked up at them. It blinked twice.

J.P. grabbed Lexie's hand.

"Earthling," J.P. said. He pointed to himself. "Nice earthling."

The creature blinked again.

"*Peaceful* earthling."

Lexie giggled. "I don't think he's going to hurt us," she said. "He looks sleepy."

"Me to be excused," the alien said. "Time of nap."

"Nap time? Wait!" Lexie cried. "You can't go back to sleep. Who are you?"

"Me Bork," he said. He closed his eyes.

"Wait!" Lexie said again. "Don't you have

anything to say to us? Like 'Take me to your leader'?"

Bork opened his eyes and yawned. "Bork say, Good gugentocks." He rubbed his stomach.

Lexie frowned. "Those were not gugentocks, those were Twinkies, and they were *mine*."

"You are thanked," said Bork.

"Where are you from?" J.P. asked.

Bork pointed to the sky. "Jum Jum," he said.

"Jum Jum?" J.P. scratched his head. "We never learned that one in our science unit."

"Why are you here?" Lexie asked.

"Bork in vacation."

"You're on a vacation?" J.P. said.

"Like earth planet. Like food of junk."

"Junk food." Lexie laughed. "Gugentocks?" she asked Bork.

He nodded and patted his stomach.

"What are you doing here?"

Bork sat up. "Me rented," he said.

"Oooooo boy," J.P. said. "Remember the sign? 'Alien for rent. Two gugentocks per hour.' "

"We hired you?" Lexie said to the alien. "With Twinkies?"

"Bork rented," he said. "Bork do work. Work done."

"What work?"

"Three works Bork do," he said. "Now Bork rest." He closed his eyes.

"Wait," said Lexie. "What works did you do?"

Bork sighed and opened his mouth. Lexie's own voice came out like a tape recording.

Somebody stop him!

"That's my voice," said Lexie. "How did you do that?" She stepped back and stared at the alien. "I said that when Bruce was going to hit J.P. That was when Bruce stopped and froze."

The alien smiled. "Good Bork. Good work."

"You saved me, Bork," J.P. said. "Good Bork. Great Bork. Wonderful Bork. Terrific Bork."

"Wow," Lexie said. "That *was* great work. But that's only one. You said you did three."

The alien closed his eyes and opened his mouth again.

Go away. Lexie's voice came out of his mouth.

"I said that to Bruce," Lexie said. "And he went away."

J.P. nodded. "Good work, Bork," he said. "You earned those gugentocks."

"Wait a minute," said Lexie. "What about number three? I didn't say anything else." She paused a moment. "Did I?"

Bork closed his eyes. He opened his mouth. Lexie's voice came out again.

You're the baby! her voice said.

"I said that to Bruce!" she said. "I said Bruce was a baby."

J.P. grabbed her arm. "You don't think he did something to Bruce?" he said.

"What did you do?" Lexie asked Bork.

"You say, I do." The alien closed his eyes again. "Now time of nap," he said, and he slowly faded away until only a green glow was left on the peanut butter sandwich.

"Come back," Lexie said. "Don't go yet."

There was no answer. The alien was gone.

"We've got to find Bruce," said Lexie. "Maybe he's on the ball field."

"*Find* Bruce?" said J.P. "We've spent all year *avoiding* Bruce."

"If the alien did something to Bruce, it's our fault," Lexie said. "We need to see if he's okay."

"I'm sure he's fine," J.P. said.

Lexie didn't answer. She picked up her lunch box and ran toward the ball field. J.P. sighed and followed her.

They checked the field. No Bruce.

"How about the basketball hoop?" No Bruce.

"Where else could he have gone?" Lexie asked. "The only place we haven't checked is the kindergarten play area." She couldn't imagine Bruce in with the little kids.

"We've got to find him."

"*Waaaaaaaaaaaaaaaaa!*"

From the play area came a loud cry. It sounded a lot like Bruce but a lot like a baby too.

"Oooo boy," said J.P. "I think we just found him."

5

Pucker Up

Lexie and J.P. ran over to the play area. They found Bruce sitting on the ground. A group of little kids was standing around staring at him.

"He looks the same!" J.P. said. Bruce still had the purple streak and the shirt that said BE AFRAID. J.P. let out a deep breath. "Good."

"He *looks* the same," said Lexie. "But he's not acting the same."

Bruce was sitting on the ground. There was dirt on his face. Tears made tracks in the dirt.

"Booboo," he said.

"His voice sounds the same," J.P. said hopefully.

"Waaaaa!" Bruce cried more loudly. "Boo-booooooo!"

"His voice sounds the same," said Lexie. "It's what he's saying that's different."

Lexie looked at J.P. "Bork did it. He really did it. He turned Bruce into a baby."

"Oooo boy," said J.P. "A baby bully."

"Waaaaaa!"

A few older kids from across the playground turned to watch.

"What's wrong with Bruce?" a boy called out.

"What did you guys do to him?" a girl asked.

"It's nothing!" Lexie called back.

"What are we going to do?" J.P. whispered. "Everyone is starting to notice."

"Waaaaaaa!" Bruce was louder now. More kids were gathering.

"Well," said Lexie, "you quiet him down. I'll get Bork to change him back."

"Boobooooooo!" Bruce was standing up, holding his finger.

"It's okay, Brucie." Lexie patted him on the

back. She looked at his outstretched finger. "He has a little cut on his finger," she said to J.P. "Take care of him."

Bruce held his finger out. J.P. looked at the cut. "Very nice," he said.

"Make all better."

"What?" J.P. backed up a few steps. "What does he want?"

"He wants you to kiss it," Lexie said. "My mom always kisses my brother's booboos."

"That's gross!"

Bruce's eyes started to fill with tears again. He took two deep breaths.

"That's disgusting."

"Just do it, J.P. We're attracting too much attention."

Lexie stepped away and opened her lunch box just a crack. "Bork?" she whispered. "Come out."

No answer.

"Bork?" she said more loudly. "We need you."

She opened the lunch box all the way. She

looked through the empty wrappers and under the sandwich. Nothing.

"Waaaaaaaa!" Bruce wailed.

Two kindergarten kids started to cry. "You're upsetting the little kids," said Lexie. "Kiss it."

"That's unsanitary."

"Make all better." Bruce held up his finger to J.P.

They could see the kindergarten teacher hurrying over to the group.

"We're out of time," said Lexie. "Pucker up."

J.P. puckered. J.P. kissed. Then he spit a few times on the ground.

"A person could die from that," he said.

"It's not that bad," Lexie said. "If you could die from kissing booboos every mother on earth would be dead."

Mr. Cleaver came out of the school and blew the whistle.

"I'm going in," said J.P. He looked nervously at the school building. "I've never been late before."

"What about him?" Lexie whispered.

"*ABCDEFG,*" Bruce sang loudly. He rocked back and forth as he sang.

"Oh, brother," J.P. said. "We can't leave him here?"

"*HIJK Limo pee.*"

"No," said Lexie. "He's a baby, remember."

"So?"

"*Q Arrest.*"

"He could get hurt."

"*T you me. Nowa said my ABC's. Dis time won't you sing with me?*"

"Come on, J.P. We can't leave a defenseless baby out on the playground alone. Let's get him inside and get him settled. Then we need to find that alien."

"That baby is not defenseless!"

Bruce finished the song with his arms spread wide. "Now you sing." He pointed to J.P.

"I'll help you get him inside," J.P. said. "But I'm not singing."

They wiped Bruce's face.

"There," said Lexie. "Time to go bye-bye."

Bruce frowned. "Sing," he commanded J.P.

They could see Mr. Cleaver looking their way. He waved his arm, signaling them to come.

Lexie took Bruce's left arm. J.P. took his right arm and they pulled him toward the school.

"No." Bruce stamped his feet. "Sing."

"You are a bully," J.P. said to Bruce. "A baby bully."

The other kids were walking toward the door of the school. "You guys better hurry," a girl called.

"No singing," J.P. said firmly.

The whistle blew again. Mr. Cleaver waved again.

Bruce's bottom lip began to tremble. He took three deep breaths.

Lexie looked at J.P.

J.P. looked back.

The whistle blew one last time.

"ABCDEFG," J.P. sang, *"HIJK Limo pee . . ."*

6

Go Potty!

They walked to the school with Bruce between them. He was singing and laughing as they walked.

"What's wrong with Bruce?" a kid asked.

"Weird," said another kid.

They could see Mr. Cleaver waiting at the top of the stairs.

"Bruce is really acting strange," said J.P. "Can we take him back to class?"

Lexie hesitated. "I don't know."

"We've got to get rid of Bruce and find Bork."

J.P. thought for a moment. "What does your mother do to make your little brother behave?"

Lexie smiled. She fished around in her pocket and came out with a Tootsie Pop.

"It never fails," she said. "Candy."

She held the Tootsie Pop out in front of Bruce.

"Brucie want candy?" she said.

Bruce nodded happily. He grabbed for the sucker.

"No, no," said Lexie, "not until we go inside."

She waved the sucker in front of his face. "Can you be good?" she asked him.

He nodded his head in big motions up and down. He licked his lips. He crossed his heart with his finger.

"Can we trust him?" J.P. asked.

"We have no choice." Lexie unwrapped the sucker and put it into Bruce's mouth.

"Say thank you," she said.

"Tank ooo," he said between smacks.

"Be good," she said.

"Brucie happy," he said. "Be good." He slurped loudly on the sucker.

"We're going in now," Lexie told Bruce. She crossed her fingers and held them up for J.P. to see.

J.P. double-crossed his.

"Brucie go bye-bye," said Bruce.

J.P. sighed. "Nothing worse than this can happen," he said.

"Don't say that!" said Lexie.

"Why?"

"I hate it when you say that."

"Why?"

"Because every time you say that something worse *does* happen."

"But nothing worse than this can happen," J.P. said again. "We've made a baby bully. I've kissed a germy cut. I sang the ABC song in front of the entire third grade. Nothing worse can happen."

Lexie shook her head. "Just don't say that," she said. "Come on. Let's go in. Let's get Bruce to class and find that alien."

She took one of Bruce's arms. J.P. took the other. They started up the stairs to the school. Mr. Cleaver glared down at them from the top step. His forehead was wrinkled and his mouth was puckered. When they got to the step below Mr. Cleaver, Bruce stopped.

His eyes got big.

He held the front of his pants.

He jumped up and down.

"Brucie need to go potty," he said. Mr. Cleaver's eyebrows shot up in surprise. His mouth formed an O.

"I beg your pardon," he said.

Bruce just kept jumping.

"Now!"

7

Brub Brub

"Potty!" Bruce yelled more loudly this time. His face scrunched up. He jumped even higher.

Mr. Cleaver frowned. "That is not amusing, Bruce."

"Potty!"

"We don't need rudeness."

"*Potty!*"

Lexie stepped up beside Bruce. "Bruce is not himself today," she said.

"I can see that," said Mr. Cleaver. "Will you and J.P. take him to the school nurse?"

"Yes."

"I'll write you some hall passes." Mr. Cleaver pulled a yellow pad out of his pocket. He wrote on three sheets and tore them off.

"You'd better hurry," he said. "Bruce is turning blue. And don't be late for assembly."

They hurried past him.

"Great," Lexie said. "If there's an assembly this afternoon no one will miss us."

Lexie and J.P. took Bruce straight to the clinic.

Mrs. Davis, the nurse, was busy with a skinned knee. "Take him in there," she said, pointing to the back room.

"Potty!" Bruce yelled as they walked by her.

"That's not funny," Mrs. Davis said. "There's a bathroom in the back."

J.P. showed Bruce the bathroom. Bruce ran in. He did not come out.

Brub brub.

A sound came from the bathroom.

They waited. And waited.

Brub brub. That sound again, but no Bruce.

"What's he doing in there?" Lexie said. "You go see."

J.P. knocked on the door.

No answer.

J.P. opened the door.

Brub brub.

"Oooo boy."

Bruce sat on the bathroom floor pulling the toilet paper off the roll. With each pull the roll brubbed. A large pile of toilet paper covered the floor.

"You'd better come in here," J.P. called to Lexie.

She peeked through the doorway.

"Oh no," she said. "How can one person make such a mess?"

"One baby," J.P. corrected her.

"One great big baby."

"Come on, Brucie." Lexie pulled him up and led him out. Mrs. Davis came into the back room.

"He's not feeling well," Lexie explained. Mrs. Davis put Bruce on a cot.

"Nap," he said in a happy voice.

"Let him rest," said Mrs. Davis. "If he's not better soon I'll call his parents." She got him a blanket and pillow.

J.P. leaned out the bathroom door. His arms were full of toilet paper. It was wrapped around his neck and shoulders.

"This is not funny, young man." Mrs. Davis spotted J.P. and the toilet paper. "You should be concerned about your friend, not playing silly games in the bathroom."

"But . . . ," J.P. said. "But . . ."

J.P. had never been in trouble before. He didn't even know what to say.

"I expect you to clean up this mess right now!"

"But . . . but . . ."

"And get right back to class!"

Lexie helped J.P. clean up the toilet paper.

Bruce put his thumb in his mouth. He curled up into a ball. He closed his eyes.

J.P. and Lexie took one last look at him as they left the clinic.

"Can we leave him here?" J.P. asked Lexie.

Mrs. Davis put her finger to her lips and then pointed to the door.

Bruce snored.

"We don't have any choice," Lexie said. "He'll be fine. My brother naps for at least an hour in the afternoon."

"I hope so," said J.P. "A baby that size could do major damage."

8

Alien or Else

"How do you find an alien?" Lexie wondered.

"Are you sure he's not in your lunch box anymore?" J.P. asked.

Lexie nodded. "He's gone," she said.

"Oooo boy," J.P. said. "If we can't find him we're sunk."

"Bruce will be a baby forever."

"And everyone will blame us."

"Let's go back to where we first found him."

"The playground?" J.P. said in a worried voice.

Lexie nodded.

"But the fourth grade is out there now. We'll get in trouble."

Lexie thought for a moment. "Where's your lunch box?"

"I left it out by the tree."

"Perfect," Lexie said. "That's a great excuse to go back out."

The hall was empty.

They hurried out the back door and ran across the playground.

"He forgot his lunch box," Lexie called out to a teacher as they ran to the tree. Lexie got to the tree first. "Come out, Bork!" she called.

No answer.

"Alien," she tried again. "Where are you?"

J.P. looked up through the branches of the tree. "I don't see anything up there. He could be any-where. He could be gone by now. He could be zipping across the sky or on some other planet."

"I hope not," Lexie said. "We've just got to find him. Or else."

"Or else what?"

"Or else Bruce stays a baby forever."

"If he *is* still here, how will we ever find him?"

"I don't know." Lexie leaned back against the tree.

"Here's your lunch box." Lexie picked up J.P.'s lunch. "Maybe he's eating yours now."

Lexie tapped the top of the lunch box.

Nothing.

She shook it a little.

Nothing.

She pulled the top open.

J.P.'s zucchini sandwich and carrot sticks were still there.

"Check yours again," J.P. said hopefully.

Nothing but Lexie's sandwich and an empty Twinkies wrapper.

"Twinkies," Lexie said. "I know he'd come out if we only had some Twinkies."

"Where are we going to get them?"

"There's nowhere to buy them at school," Lexie said. "The closest place to buy them is down the street, and we'd get caught for sure."

J.P. looked inside Lexie's lunch box. "I have an idea," he said. "Remember Tubs?"

"Your guinea pig?"

J.P. nodded. "Tubs was under the sofa one time and we couldn't get him out. He'd usually come out for lettuce, but we were out of lettuce."

"So?"

"So we crinkled the lettuce wrapper, and when he heard the sound he ran out."

Lexie looked down at the lunch box and the empty Twinkies wrapper.

"Good thinking," she said. She grabbed the wrapper and began to crinkle it.

Crinkle. Crinkle.

She crinkled it by the tree.

Crinkle. Crinkle.

She crinkled it behind the tree.

J.P. nudged her and pointed to a bush. The bush was glowing a greenish color.

Crinkle. Crinkle.

She crinkled the paper by the bush.

The bush glowed brighter.

And brighter.
And brighter.
Crinkle. Crinkle.
The branches parted and Bork leaned out.
He sniffed the air.
"Gugentocks!"

9

Arrest That Alien!

"**B**ork!"

Lexie kneeled by the bush.

"Bork!" J.P. said. "We're so glad to see you."

The little alien patted his stomach. "Gugentocks?" he said hopefully.

"Sorry," Lexie said.

Bork began to fade a little. "No gugentocks," he said in a sad voice.

"But maybe later," Lexie said quickly. "Don't go!"

"Later?" Bork returned.

Lexie nodded. "Bork," she said, "you've got to turn him back."

"Who to back?"

"Bruce to back," Lexie said.

"Back to who?"

"Back to self."

"You're talking like him," J.P. said. "Let me explain. Bork, you can't just go around turning people into babies."

Bork blinked. "Bad Bork," he said sadly. "You not like Bork work." A big tear rolled down his green cheek. "Bork go Jum Jum."

"No!" Lexie and J.P. said together. "Don't go Jum Jum!"

"We like you," Lexie added.

"Like Bork?" He stopped crying.

"We love you."

"Love Bork?" He stood up straighter.

"We love your work. But . . ." Lexie took a deep breath. "We just want Bruce to not be a baby anymore."

Bork smiled.

"Where Bruce?" he asked.

"Time of nap," J.P. said. "I hope."

"Take to Bruce. Bork fix."

Lexie picked up her lunch box. "You can ride in here," she said. She opened it up and patted the sandwich. She held the lunch box out to the bush.

Bork stepped in. He sniffed.

"No gugentocks?"

"Later," Lexie promised. "Ready?"

Bork sat down on the sandwich and nodded.

Lexie closed the lunch box and they walked quickly back to the school. Lexie held the lunch box close to her so that it wouldn't shake too much.

"I'm starving," she said. "After we get Bruce turned back we can eat lunch."

J.P. stopped suddenly.

He grabbed Lexie's arm.

"Look!" he said.

A police car was parked beside the school. Three police officers jumped out of the car and hurried into the building.

"Oh no!" J.P. said. "Can they arrest an alien?"

Lexie held the lunch box even tighter.

"Nobody's arresting this alien," she said.

10

Baby Escape

"We can't go in," J.P. said.

"We have to."

"Maybe we should just go home."

"We can't just go home in the middle of the day," said Lexie. She looked at the school and took a deep breath. "Besides, we've got to change Bruce back."

"What about the police?"

"I don't know," said Lexie. "We'll just have to avoid them."

"What about Mrs. Davis?"

"We'll just have to avoid her too."

"What about Mrs. Nugent? What about Mr. Cleaver?"

Lexie and J.P. stood and looked at the police car. "If only we were invisible," Lexie said.

Lexie felt dizzy for a second. She closed her eyes. When she opened them again J.P. was gone. "J.P.?" she said. "Where are you?"

"Wh-Wh-Wh-What?" J.P.'s voice answered. But where was he?

Lexie looked down at herself. Nothing.

"We're invisible!" she said. "Yay, Bork!"

"Where are you?" J.P. asked. "Lexie, help!"

Lexie felt around in the direction of J.P.'s voice until she touched him. "Hold my hand," she said. "So we can stay together."

They walked up the steps together, right under the nose of a fourth-grade teacher.

"She can't see us," Lexie said. Lexie stood right beside her and yelled, "Boo!"

The teacher threw her papers into the air. She looked all around and scratched her head.

Lexie and J.P. opened the door and walked into

the building. Two police officers were standing in the hall.

Lexie took a deep breath. "Be quiet," she whispered to J.P. "They can't see us, but they can hear us."

Lexie and J.P. tiptoed down the hall. The closer they got to the police officers, the closer they got to each other.

It was hard for them to walk together when they couldn't see each other. Lexie could hear J.P. breathing harder. She could hear her own heart beating.

She put one foot in front of the other. They got right in front of the police officers. Lexie's invisible foot stepped on J.P.'s invisible foot. She felt herself falling. The lunch box flew out of her hand and thudded on the floor.

"Mac?" one officer said to the other. "You hear something?"

Lexie held her breath. She felt around on the floor to find the invisible lunch box.

The officers began to look around the hall.

Lexie tried to stay out of their way. She had to find the lunch box.

"Ouch!" said J.P.'s voice.

One officer looked confused. "I stepped on something," he said. "At least I thought I did."

"Mice?" the other officer said.

"Squeak, squeak," Lexie said.

Her hand finally closed around the lunch box.

She grabbed it and ran.

Her footsteps echoed down the hall, but Lexie didn't care. J.P.'s footsteps echoed after hers.

The two officers looked down the empty hallway and shrugged.

Lexie and J.P. opened the door of the clinic. Mrs. Davis was reading a book called *Pirate's Passion* and eating Hershey's kisses. She didn't notice the door slowly creaking open.

They tiptoed to the back room.

They opened the door.

Lexie and J.P. stared. The cot was empty.

Baby Bruce was on the loose.

11

Invisible

Lexie and J.P. walked back out into the hall. The police were gone, but the hall was filled with kids walking toward the cafeteria. It was time for assembly.

Lexie and J.P. stepped back into the doorway so that no one would step on them. They were still invisible.

Lexie snatched a hat off a boy's head as he went by. She threw it into the air. The boy poked the guy next to him.

"What did you do that for?" he said.

"I didn't do anything."

"Did too."

Lexie giggled.

Mr. Cleaver walked down the hall with the kids.

"Watch this," Lexie whispered to J.P.

"Don't do it!" J.P. said. "Whatever it is, don't do it."

Mr. Cleaver got closer.

"Just wait," Lexie said.

"Don't do it, Lexie," J.P. said. He grabbed her arm.

Mr. Cleaver walked right in front of them.

"Mr. Cleaver is a sissy!" Lexie called out.

Mr. Cleaver looked in their direction.

He pointed to a group of girls that had just gone by. "You there," he said to the girls, "did you say something?"

The girls shook their heads.

"You, then." He followed another group up the hall. "Did you say something?"

"No, sir."

"You . . . you there." He followed another group.

J.P. giggled.

Finally the hall was empty.

All the classrooms were empty.

Everyone was gone.

"Now what?" said J.P. "Where do you look for a baby?"

"Babies like people," Lexie said. "Everyone is in the cafeteria."

"Bruce too?"

"Maybe. Let's see."

"Ask Bork to turn us back now," J.P. said.

As he said it, their color came back to them. First green, then all the other colors until they were visible again.

As they neared the cafeteria they heard the sound of a crowd of people. The people were laughing.

Lexie held her lunch box and walked down the hall, closer and closer to the cafeteria doors.

J.P. followed her.

"The police may be in there," he whispered.

"We've got to find Bruce," Lexie answered.

They reached the doors and stopped.

From the microphone in the cafeteria they heard a voice. The voice had to be coming from the stage. It was Bruce's voice.

"Oh no," said Lexie.

Bruce was singing.

" 'I'm a little teapot, short and stout.' "

12

Don't Die

"I 'm going to die," said J.P.

"Don't die," Lexie said.

"Then I'm going to faint."

"You're not going to faint."

"Then what am I going to do?"

"You're going to stand in front of me and hide my lunch box."

Lexie stood behind J.P. in the doorway.

They could see the crowds of kids sitting on folding chairs watching the stage. They could see the teachers standing on the sides looking at

Bruce. They could sec a police officer behind Bruce on the stage and three more in the front row. They could see Mr. Cleaver frowning in the back of the room.

Lexie opened the lunch box lid a crack.

"Change him back," she whispered. "He's there. On the stage."

Bork shook his head.

"Change him back," said Lexie. "Right now."

"Closer," Bork said.

"Closer!" J.P. looked at the stage. "He wants to go closer!" J.P.'s voice got higher when he said the word *closer*. "Now I know I'm going to die."

"You're not."

"Or at least faint."

"You can't."

Lexie grabbed his arm.

"You can die and faint later. Right now we are going up on that stage."

"Oooo boy!"

They walked slowly toward the stage. The closer

they got to the stage, the quieter the crowd became. Then they climbed up the steps to where Bruce stood.

Lexie stood on one side of Bruce. J.P. stood on the other. They stared out at the crowd. Everyone had been quiet at first; now they were whispering.

"What's going on?"

"What are they doing up there?"

"Well," J.P. whispered. "What now?" He looked out at the kids. He looked at the teachers and the police officers sitting in the front row.

Lexie didn't answer. She looked behind them to see the other police officer making his way to the front of the stage. In front of her she could see Mr. Cleaver walking toward the stage.

" 'Tip me over and pour me out,' " sang Bruce as he bent to the side. One arm was up like a teapot spout, the other making a handle on his hip.

"Now," said Lexie to her lunch box.

"Fix now?" Bork said.

"Quick!"

Mr. Cleaver was almost at the stage.

"Go!"

Bork blinked.

Brucc glowed green.

He rose slightly from the stage. His body shook a little. His eyes got big. Then he dropped back down.

There were gasps from the crowd. Lexie stared out at the surprised faces. Mrs. Nugent's mouth was hanging open.

Bruce put his hand to his head and stared at the crowd.

"What?" he said. "Where? How?"

Lexie stood in front of the whole school, Mr. Cleaver, all the kids, and four police officers, and for once in her life she could think of nothing to say.

"You can faint now," she said to J.P.

13

Just Say Bork

The crowd got very quiet.

Everyone stared at J.P. and Lexie and Bruce.

Lexie looked at the police officer behind her. She noticed that he was holding a poster. The poster said JUST SAY NO TO DRUGS.

She nudged J.P.

"I think I've got an idea," she said.

Lexie stepped forward to the microphone. Bruce had not moved. He looked as if he was still in shock. Mr. Cleaver frowned up at her from below.

"We just wanted to show you . . . ," Lexie began. The microphone whined a little. She caught her breath. "That you act like a baby if you do drugs."

Everyone was silent. Lexie looked at J.P. "Help," she mouthed.

"So," said J.P. He stepped up beside her. "Don't use drugs."

Everyone began to clap. The police officers clapped. The teachers clapped. Lexie noticed that Mr. Cleaver did not clap.

Bruce blinked.

"What?" he said. "Where? How?"

"Show's over, Brucie," said Lexie. She grabbed his arm and led him off the stage. Mr. Cleaver blocked the door.

"Not so fast," he said.

They stopped and looked at him. Lexie held her lunch box tighter.

Mr. Cleaver stared at them for a moment.

"You three have been up to something." He crossed his arms.

"We have?" J.P. said.

Mr. Cleaver nodded.

"You three have really surprised me today."

"We have?" J.P.'s voice was higher.

Mr. Cleaver rubbed his chin.

Lexie and J.P. and Bruce stood and stared at Mr. Cleaver.

What was the punishment for turning someone into a baby? For hiding an alien? For becoming invisible? J.P. wondered.

Mr. Cleaver smiled.

"Very nice presentation, Lexie and J.P. And Bruce, nice to see you participating." He shook their hands.

"It was?" J.P. said.

"What?" Bruce said. "Where?"

Lexie grinned.

"It was *very* nice," said Mr. Cleaver. "Glad to see your hard work. I'm going to give you extra credit in English."

"Huh?" Bruce said. He had never gotten extra credit in anything.

"And I liked the special effects."

"Thank you," said Lexie.

"Thank you," said J.P.

"Tank ooo," said Bruce. Lexie and J.P. stared at him. Mr. Cleaver looked surprised. "I mean thank you," Bruce said.

Lexie and J.P. laughed.

14

Gugentocks

The bell rang. School was over.

Lexie took her lunch box and walked slowly back to the oak tree. J.P. made a quick stop down the street and returned with a brown paper bag.

Bork sat on top of the lunch box.

"Good work?" Bork asked.

"Great work," J.P. said. "Terrific work."

He opened the brown paper bag and pulled out three packs of Twinkies.

"Have a gugentock," he said.

"Gugentocks! *MMMMMMMmmmm.*"

Bork smiled contentedly and took the Twinkie.

Lexie shook her head and smiled. "Gugentocks," she said happily. She opened a pack and took a bite. "I guess this is lunch."

"Gugentocks." J.P. laughed and pulled his pack open. "This beats a zucchini sandwich." He turned to Bork. "Tomorrow we'll introduce you to Moon Pies."

Bork looked up, cream covering his little face.

"Bork go many vacations. Many gugentocks. Many Pies of Moon."

Lexie laughed. "You can come see us anytime you want," she said.

"More works?" he asked.

"Please, Bork," J.P. said. He laughed. "That was enough. Please, no more works."

"Never?" Bork asked.

J.P. looked at Lexie.

Lexie grinned. "Well . . ."

"I mean, think of what could have happened," J.P. said.

"Well . . ."

"I mean, look at all the trouble we could have gotten into."

"Well . . ."

"What would my mother say?"

Lexie laughed and smiled at Bork. "I never say never," she said. "You don't know when we might need a little help from a little friend."

Bork smiled. "Just call Bork," he said. He finished the last bite of his Twinkie and slowly faded away.

J.P. leaned back against the tree and shook his head.

"Oooo boy!"

About the Author

Betsy Duffey lives in Atlanta with her husband and two sons. She encountered her first bully in the first grade when a fifth-grade boy tried to put her into a trash can at recess. He was not successful. Betsy Duffey writes authentically about the concerns of elementary-school children by remembering her childhood and watching her own children grow up. This is her twentieth book for young readers.